Disney
Olaf's FROZEN ADVENTURE

by AMY SKY KOSTER

Illustrated by the DISNEY STORYBOOK ART TEAM

Olaf burst out of a KRANSEKAKE, with pieces of the cake made out of rings flying everywhere.

"Surprise!" he shouted.

"Olaf, not yet!" said Anna.

Elsa smiled. "The surprise holiday party starts *after* the Yule Bell rings."

It was Arendelle's first holiday season in forever, and the two sisters would be spending it together with their kingdom.

The castle courtyard was filled with festive townspeople. Everyone had been excited as Kristoff and Sven brought in the Yule Bell.

"The Yule Bell signals the start of the holidays in Arendelle!" Elsa told Olaf.

"Okay, now," Anna whispered.

Bong! Bong! Bong! The bell rang out and all the villagers cheered!

"SURPRISE!" shouted Olaf to the crowd.

And with that, Elsa and Anna flung open the doors to the castle to invite everyone in. But instead of staying for the surprise party, the townspeople started to LEAVE!

"WAIT!" Anna said. "Going so soon?"

One woman replied, "The Yule Bell rang, so I must get home for my family's tradition: rolling the *lefse*!"

Two sisters explained, "We're baking traditional *bordstabelbakkels*!"

Everybody sounded very busy rolling their special bread and baking festive biscuits. Next, Elsa invited Mr and Mrs Olsen to the castle, but they also shook their heads.

"Thank you, but Olga and I need to get home to knit SOCKS for our grandchildren." Old Roy smiled. "We wouldn't want to intrude on your family traditions."

With the villagers gone, the sisters needed cheering up. Kristoff serenaded them with his holiday tradition from the trolls, "THE BALLAD OF FLEMINGRAD." But the song took a strange turn when Kristoff started singing about NOSTRILS.

Then Kristoff revealed another troll tradition: FLEMMY THE FUNGUS TROLL!

"Woah, gross," said Anna.

"Now you lick his forehead and make a wish!" Kristoff said.

Everyone laughed.

Olaf followed the sisters into the ballroom. He couldn't WAIT to hear what Anna and Elsa's holiday tradition was. "Do we have any traditions, Elsa?" asked Anna. "Do you remember?"

"After the gates were closed, we were never together," Elsa replied. "I'm sorry, Anna. It's MY fault that we don't have a tradition."

Over the past few months, Olaf had learnt a little about why certain events and items were important to different people. And now he understood something new: EVERYONE in Arendelle had a holiday tradition. Everyone EXCEPT Anna and Elsa.

Olaf ran to the stable.

"Sven! Anna and Elsa don't have a holiday tradition." Then he had an idea. "Let's go and FIND the best tradition Anna and Elsa have ever seen and bring it back to the castle!"

Olaf hooked Sven to Kristoff's sleigh and the two immediately set off.

Olaf knocked on the door of the first house they came to.

"What is your holiday tradition?" Olaf asked a young boy and his mother.

"We make **CANDY CANES** together." The boy handed one to Olaf.

Olaf pulled out his carrot nose and popped in the candy cane. His eyes whirled.

"OHHH, SUGAR RUSH!"

The boy stared at Olaf. "You're supposed to eat it."

"Eat my new nose? Why would I do that?" asked Olaf.

"Because it's that time of year!" the boy said.

Olaf and Sven stopped at HOME after HOME to learn about different holiday traditions.

They loaded all the traditions onto SVEN'S SLEIGH,
so they could take them back to Anna and Elsa.

At their last stop, Olaf found the entire OAKEN family celebrating in the sauna. Olaf thought that was a great tradition…

… and added a PORTABLE SAUNA to the pile!

But **HOT COALS** from the sauna caused problems.
The sleigh caught fire and the traditions began to burn!
When the sleigh went over a cliff, Sven and Olaf landed on
opposite sides of a ravine…

... and THE HOLIDAY TRADITIONS WERE GONE!

Olaf was still hopeful because he had one last tradition, a fruitcake, that he could give Anna and Elsa.

But Sven was worried. He could hear WOLVES howling in the dark forest.

Back at the castle, Elsa found Anna in the **ATTIC**.

"What are you doing up here?" asked Elsa.

"Looking for **TRADITIONS**," said Anna. She had been pulling items out of a trunk filled with her childhood belongings.

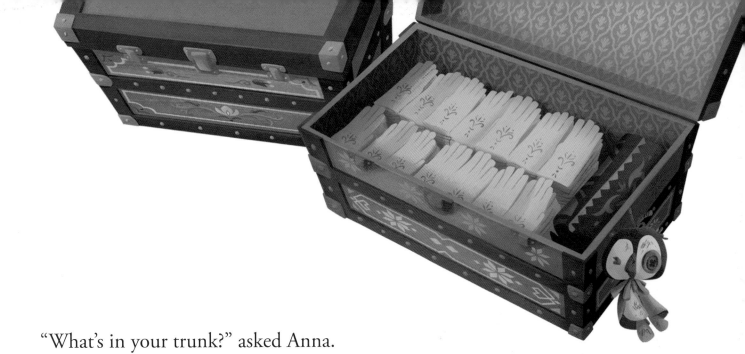

"What's in your trunk?" asked Anna.

"Mostly GLOVES," said Elsa.

But as Elsa reached inside her trunk, they heard a little bell ring.

Elsa lifted out a small box and handed it to Anna. When Anna opened it, SHE COULDN'T BELIEVE HER EYES.

Suddenly, the two sisters heard a KERFUFFLE outside.
They ran down to the stables, where Sven was trying to
tell Kristoff something.

"Olaf is LOST in the forest!" said Anna.

"And being chased by HUNGRY WOLVES!" said Elsa.

The sisters knew they needed to gather EVERYONE and
search for Olaf right away.

Anna and Elsa headed INTO THE FOREST, calling out
Olaf's name. Kristoff and Sven were close behind with a search
party of villagers.

"OLAF, WHERE ARE YOU?" called a worried Anna.

Just when they thought they might never find him, the sisters
spotted a carrot sticking out of a snowdrift – Olaf!

Olaf explained how he had lost all the traditions he'd
collected for his friends. Even the FRUITCAKE, which had
been grabbed by a bird!

"I'm sorry you still don't have a tradition," the little snowman said.

"OLAF, WE DO. LOOK," said Anna.

She opened the mystery box and showed Olaf what was inside.

The box was filled with SKETCHES ANNA HAD MADE OF OLAF when she was a little girl!

"You're the one who first brought us together," said Anna.

"And kept us connected when we were apart," added Elsa.

"EVERY Christmas, I made Elsa a gift," Anna continued.

Elsa nodded. "All those long years alone, we had you to remind us of our childhood."

"And of how much we still LOVED each other," Anna agreed.

"It's you, Olaf. YOU are our holiday tradition," said Anna. "SURPRISE!"

GLOWING LANTERNS emerged from the dark forest.
The townspeople were relieved to see that Olaf was safe.
That's when Elsa had a BRILLIANT IDEA.

Because this was Anna and Elsa's FIRST WINTER HOLIDAY in forever,
the celebration needed to be special. With a little help from the villagers, they
hosted their big party after all, right there in the forest!

Best of all, Anna and Elsa rediscovered their
HOLIDAY TRADITION, and a new one was
created for Arendelle. All thanks to OLAF.